The Blossom Shoppe

By Katherine & Caroline Brickley
Illustrated by Joanie Stone

The Blossom Co.

Published in the United States by The Blossom Company, Connecticut,
a subsidiary of Happily Ever After, LLC.
The Blossom Company and design are registered trademarks and associated logos are
trademarks and/or registered trademarks of Happily Ever After, LLC.

Library of Congress Cataloging-in-Publication Data
The Blossom Shoppe/Katherine Brickley and Caroline Brickley;
illustrated by Joanie Stone
Summary: The heartwarming story of twin sisters Poppy and Posie Blossom
and their unforgettable journey to save the Blossom Shoppe.
ISBN 978-0-9977827-0-7 (trade)
ISBN 978-0-9977827-2-1 (ebook)
[1. Sisters—Fiction. 2. Flowers—Fiction. 3. Being yourself—Fiction.].
10 9 8 7 6 5 4 3 2 1

First Edition

Printed in China

Visit us on the Web at www.blossomcompanyct.com

For family, friends, and flowers.
—Katherine & Caroline

To my parents, Sherry and Roger,
for always believing in my dream.
—Joanie

In a town so dull and gray it even lacked a name, twin sisters Poppy and Posie Blossom lived above their family flower shop. The rest of the town thought flowers were frivolous, but to the Blossoms, they were anything but. The Blossom Shoppe was their home, and their flowers were family.

Blossom Shoppe

Their flowers . . .
. . . made them smile . . .
. . . brightened up the grayest of days . . .
. . . and were the perfect gifts to share.
If only everyone else in the town knew just what a flower could do.

One Monday morning, Poppy twirled around
the shop, waking each flower with a splash of
water, while Posie placed bouquets outside, hoping
to draw customers in.

"What would I do without you, my little sprouts?"
Mama Blossom asked. She tucked flowers behind their
ears and sent them off to school.

On their way they passed:

Gary the grocer, selling his forlorn fruits and veggies.

Danielle the dog walker, guiding a group of gray dogs.

Patrick the postman, driving his mopey mail truck.

And Denise the dressmaker, sewing her drab-ulous dresses . . .

"Here come those Blossom girls," Denise whispered to her customer as her grumpy puppy growled. "Their mother owns that silly flower shop, and now she's begun to dress them up like flowers too! When will they realize their little Blossom Shoppe will never be in fashion?"

As the sisters approached, Denise stopped her gossiping to wish them "a very gray day."

Poppy and Posie politely wished her the same, but they really hoped for more than just another gray day.

At school, while sitting in Ms. Mousy's math class, Poppy and Posie couldn't help but daydream about what a day without gray would be like.

Could such a day even exist?

Eager to ask Mama Blossom, they hurried home from school. But when they arrived, they were astonished to find . . .

The flower shop was empty, with a "For Sale" sign right out front!

Blossom Shoppe

For Sale

Raymond Realtors

"My dearest sprouts," Mama Blossom said, hugging them tight, "we are going to have to sell the shop. We just can't afford to keep it open anymore. It seems our shop doesn't fit very well in a town so dull and gray."

Poppy and Posie were heartbroken. They couldn't bear to be without their Blossom Shoppe. If only the town was able to see all that their flowers could do, the sisters were certain they could save it.

But how could Poppy and Posie show them?

Then, they thought of it: They would grow the most fantastic flower in the world.

Poppy and Posie searched every inch of the shop for a seed, but not a single one could be found.

That's when they remembered the flowers Mama Blossom had given them that morning. They gently shook the flowers, and tiny seeds fell into their hands.

They appeared to be just ordinary gray seeds, but under the girls' touch the seeds began to glisten and glow in colors they had never seen before!

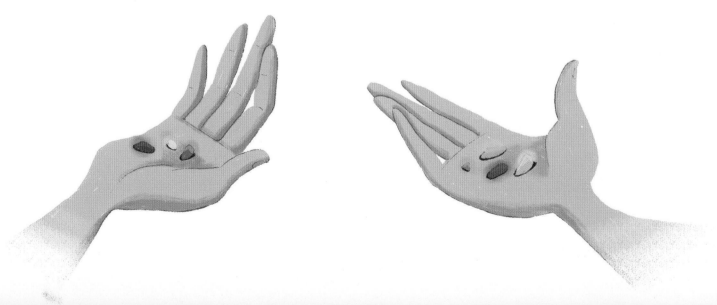

Poppy and Posie planted the seeds in front of the shop where
the sun shone the brightest. They watered them, tucked them
under a blanket of straw, and sang them a good-night lullaby.

That night, when Poppy and Posie fell asleep, they were met
with dreams full of color.

But when they awoke the next morning, it appeared to be just another gray day.

That is, until they looked at each other and discovered . . .

their cheeks were powder pink!

And when they went outside, a
tiny sprout was there to greet them.

Each day that week, Poppy and Posie became more and more colorful. And with their love and care, the sprout slowly grew.

On Wednesday, they awoke to find their nails painted in shimmering shades, and their sprout had grown its first leaf.

On Thursday, Poppy and Posie's hair burst with color the moment they brushed through it, and their sprout had begun to bud.

While the sisters were delighted at the new colors they were discovering each day, they feared what others might think or say. So they hid their transformation.

But by Friday, they could hide no more. Poppy and Posie were both as brilliant as a box of crayons!

Their sprout, however, was still very small and very, *very* gray. They wondered if it would ever blossom.

Poppy and Posie caused quite a commotion as they walked to school that day.

And when they got there, the students went gray-zy!

Ms. Mousy, annoyed by the disruption, sent the girls
home with a note for their mother.

At home, Poppy and Posie were met with an even greater predicament. Their sprout had still not blossomed, and even worse, Mr. Raymond the Realtor was selling their shop . . . to Denise!

Mr. Raymond handed Mama Blossom a piece of paper and said, "Now if you would just sign right here . . ."

The sisters rushed to the sprout. "Please bloom," they pleaded, but it didn't budge.

Poppy and Posie's eyes overflowed with rainbow tears.

The sprout *still* didn't budge.

Then Poppy had an idea. She wiped away her tears and said, "What if . . ." Before she could finish, Posie was nodding.

Together, they threw away their drab disguises. For the first time they did not worry about what others might think or say. Touching the bud, they imagined it shining with color, just like them.

Suddenly, the sprout changed from gray to green and grew taller and taller.

Denise ran away.

Mr. Raymond fainted.

Mama Blossom gasped in surprise.

"This is awesome!" Poppy exclaimed.

"No, this is . . .

"BLOSSOM!" Posie cheered.
The magnificent flower shone with colors just
as bright as Poppy and Posie . . .

. . . and soon the town did too!

Curious and newly colorful people gathered outside the shop.
Upon seeing the most fantastic flower ever grown, they all lined
up to buy a one-of-a-kind blossom of their very own. To Poppy
and Posie's surprise, Denise was first in line.

With so much business, the Blossoms were able to save their
beloved Blossom Shoppe, which was now beloved by all.

The entire town was bursting with color and
blooming with happiness! Because of
Poppy and Posie, everyone finally
knew just what a flower could do.
And because of a flower, Poppy and Posie
now knew all that *they* could do.

The End